This Little Tiger
book belongs to:

_____

_____

_____

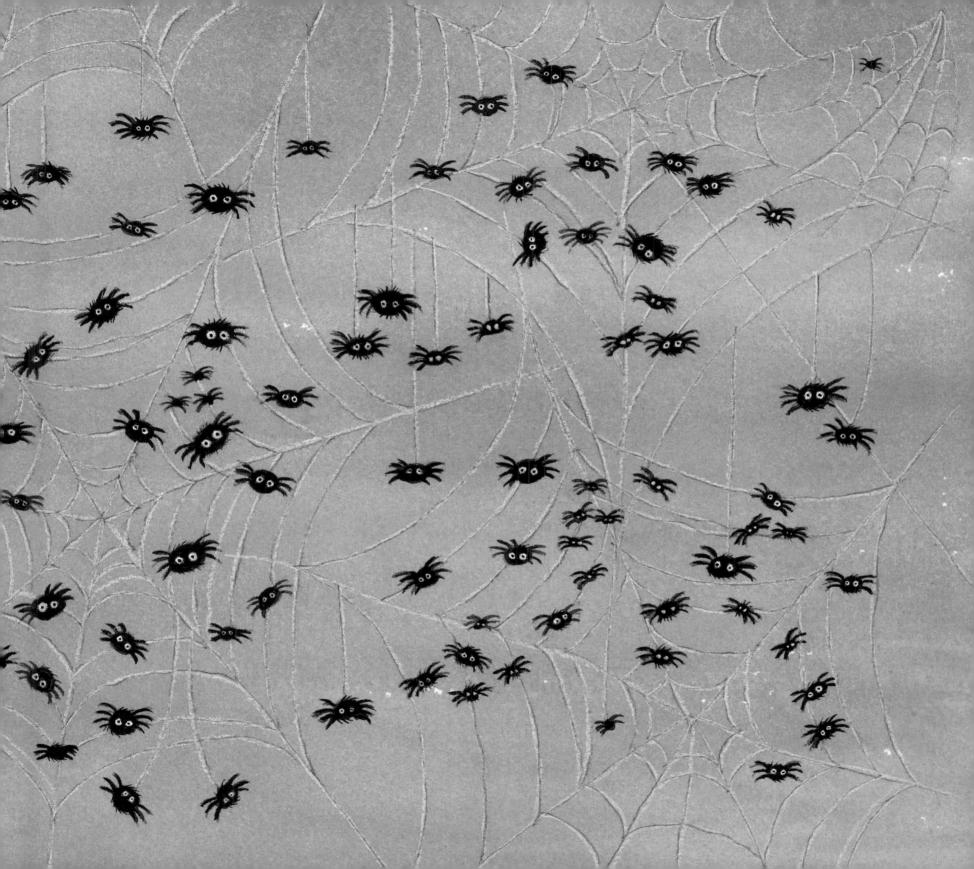

For Eva and *her* witch, with thanks
– L M

Pour Pruno, dont les histoires extraordinaires
faisaient fuir nos peurs d'enfants
– J D

LITTLE TIGER PRESS
An imprint of Magi Publications
1 The Coda Centre, 189 Munster Road, London SW6 6AW
www.littletigerpress.com

First published in Great Britain 2005
This edition published 2005

Printed in Belgium by Proost N.V.

2 4 6 8 10 9 7 5 3 1

The Witch With a Twitch

Layn Marlow

Joelle Dreidemy

LITTLE TIGER PRESS
London

Kitch was an ordinary witch's cat.
But his beloved mistress, Willa, was
no ordinary witch.

ITCHING POWDER

TASTE IT!

delicious
eyes

magic

The rest of the coven called
her cowardy custard, and even Kitch
had to admit his witch was a bit of
a scaredy-cat.

and spiders made her jump out of her skin!

Screech!

Willa was a very twitchy witch, which could only spell trouble for Kitch.

One dark night, Willa and Kitch were zooming through the sky on the broom.

Willa was already
feeling twitchy
in the darkness,
but suddenly . . .

Oh no! An owl!
What a fright!
The witch twitched,
the broomstick pitched,

Aaaah!

and Kitch ended up in the mud!

Splat!

Poor Kitch!

Willa took him home for a special bath.
Just two drops of magic potion would
cast a spell to make Kitch's fur shiny
and sleek again. Drip, drip . . .

Oh no! A mouse!
The witch twitched,
the spell switched,

and Kitch found
himself covered in spots!
He looked ridiculous.

Squeak!
Squeak!

Poor, spotty Kitch spent that night trying to hide. But he was soon discovered by the other coven cats.

They teased him till Kitch could stand it no more.

LOST
SWEETY

please call
0331894701

MEG
SHOE

He made up his mind
to go away to sea.

Dear Willa,
Gone to be a
ship's cat.

Meanwhile, Willa searched all night for the spell to put Kitch right.

Finally she found it and hurried to cure her spotty cat.

But all she spotted was his note.
Willa was very upset. Kitch had
gone! She had to find him!

Willa flew high and
low looking for Kitch,

but simply couldn't find him
anywhere . . .

until at last she spied a tiny boat being
tossed about on the stormy sea.
In the boat was a sickly-looking Kitch.
He was overjoyed to see Willa again.

The witch raised her wand to cast a
calming spell on the water, but suddenly . . .

...a **gigantic** whale rose out of the ocean!
What a shock!

The boat dipped and Kitch fell
right into the deep, cold water!
Splash!
He had never been so afraid.
Now Kitch was in real danger!

Without the slightest twitch,
Willa dodged the whale,

braved the waves,

and hauled her dear cat
to safety on the broom.

Back home the witch magicked the spots away and fussed over her cat until he felt better.

Now Willa didn't give two hoots about swooping owls, or snooping mice, or even scary spiders! Kitch was safe and sound and very proud of his own dear, kind, BRAVE witch.

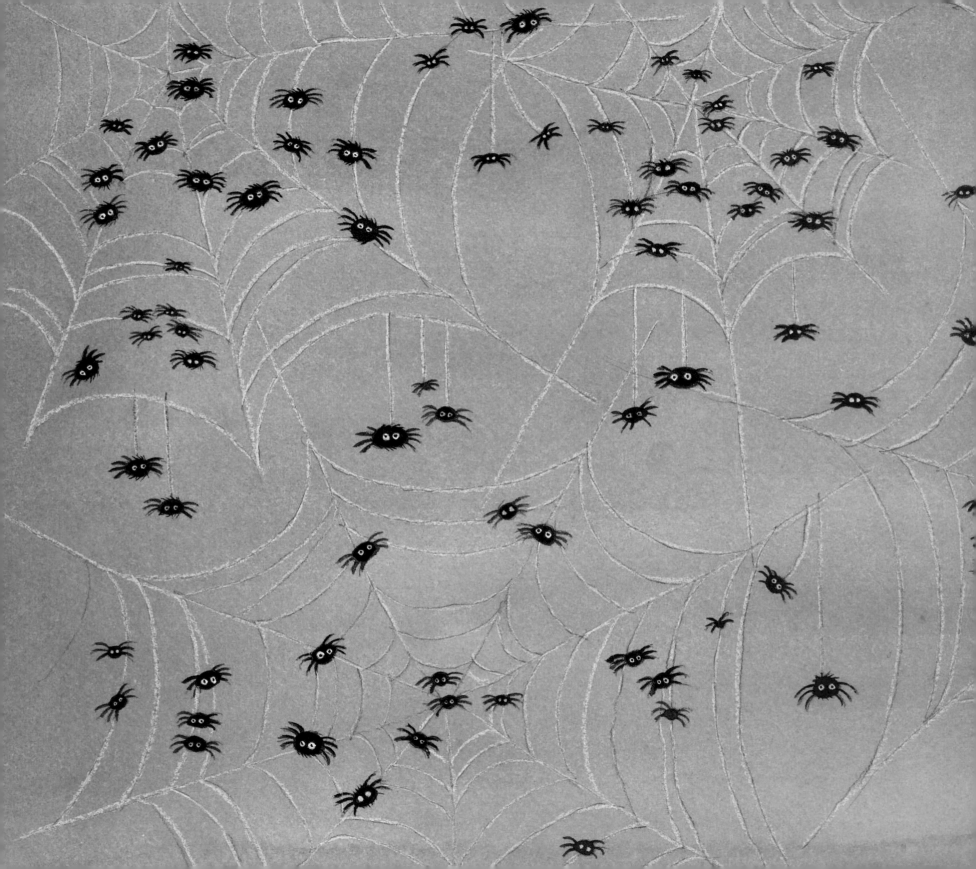

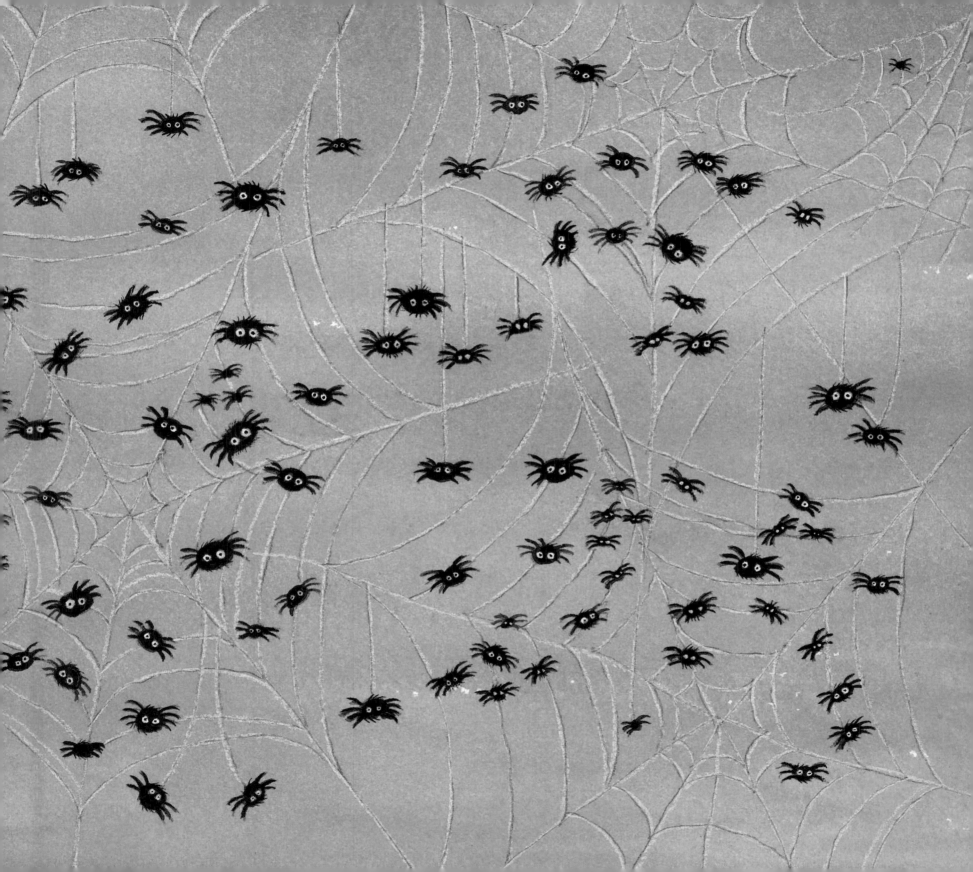

Bored Bill
Liz Pichon

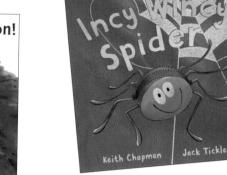

Nobody Laughs at a Lion!
Paul Bright   Illustrated by Matt Buckingham

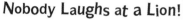

Incy Wincy Spider
Keith Chapman   Jack Tickle

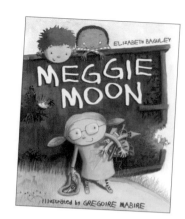

ELIZABETH BAGULEY
MEGGIE MOON
Illustrated by GREGOIRE MABIRE

More magical reads from Little Tiger Press

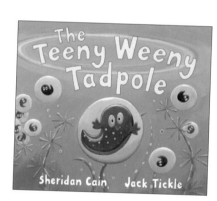

The Teeny Weeny Tadpole
Sheridan Cain   Jack Tickle

Too Busy for Benjie
Christine Leeson
Andy Ellis

For information regarding any of the above
titles or for our catalogue, please contact us:
Little Tiger Press, 1 The Coda Centre,
189 Munster Road, London SW6 6AW
Tel: 020 7385 6333 Fax: 020 7385 7333
E-mail: info@littletiger.co.uk
www.littletigerpress.com